Bill & Carolyn,
Happy Reading,
Happy adventures,
Happy Smiles,
Much love, blessings
and prayers
Glenda, Don & Johnny Bob

Glenda Buckmier

A Horse Goes to the Store

Johnny Bob Adventures

Archway Publishing books may be ordered through booksellers or by contacting:

Archway Publishing
1663 Liberty Drive
Bloomington, IN 47403
www.archwaypublishing.com
1 (888) 242-5904

ISBN: 978-1-4808-4576-3 (sc)
ISBN: 978-1-4808-4577-0 (hc)
ISBN: 978-1-4808-4578-7 (e)

Library of Congress Control Number: 2017906396

Print information available on the last page.

Archway Publishing rev. date: 8/29/2017

For Don, Michael, Megan
Master Story Teller Johnny Bob—age six years—
and Dusty.
You inspire me!

Once upon a time, there was a horse named Dusty who lived on Farmer Bill Green's farm. Farmer Bill's farm was a happy, busy working farm. Farmer Bill had dairy cows and grew wheat and oats. Trees lined the main road into the farm. There were pastures, creeks, rolling hills, and white fences.

All kinds of farm equipment were housed in a red garage. The farmhands lived in red bunkhouses. A cookhouse with lots of windows was open to everyone who lived on the farm. There was a large brass bell with a long rope that the cook rang for meals.

Breakfast was served early for the farmhands. Bacon, eggs, fluffy biscuits, pancakes, waffles, tomatoes, onions, peppers, watermelon, cantaloupe, and strawberries from the garden were just a few of the breakfast items the farmhands consumed before heading out to work on the farm with their yummy snacks in brown paper bags. Lunch and dinner were also prepared, and snacks were available all day long.

The large red weathered barn had a black roof and a dozen stalls. Dusty's stall, number one, was the largest, with a double door that could be opened from the top or the bottom. He got his mail in his own personal mailbox outside his stall. The mailman brought his mail and he always honked his horn so Dusty would know he had mail even if he was out in the pasture.

Dusty was a happy horse who loved to eat, work, play, and sleep. He liked long rides in the pasture, splashing in the creek, wearing pretty shoes, and eating delicious red apples and long orange carrots with green frilly tops. He loved to shop and was always eager to read the Everything Store flyers that he found in his mailbox. He would dance around and lay out the flyers and take a long look at the pretty shoes, apples, carrots, and SnickerPoodles, an all-natural animal treat for the cat and dog. He liked to read the newspaper and window shop because he hadn't gotten the hang of the computer and online shopping. His feet just couldn't quite make the keys work right.

After a day of work and play, he took his shoes off and played a long game of cards with the cat, Theodora, and the dog, Suzy Q, who lived in the barn.

Theodora liked to wear bright pink collars with her black fur coat. She had a white marking between her eyes and a long tail that rubbed against Farmer Bill's legs. She loved to be petted and took long naps in the sun.

Suzy Q was a black and white miniature schnauzer who loved to run and play. She sported a red leather collar. She loved to walk with Dusty to the creek near the barn or ride with her head hanging out of the window, directing the way as a copilot in Farmer Bill's pickup. Suzy Q had a special place on the couch in Farmer Bill's office, where she kept an eye on Farmer Bill, ears for the farm hands, and a nose for the delicious smells coming out of the kitchen.

Dusty was usually a happy horse, but, today, he was not. His feet hurt. His shoes did not fit anymore. He needed a new pair of shoes, and he was sure he also needed some more apples, carrots, and SnickerPoodles so this meant shopping—serious shopping. Did he like to shop? Indeed, he did!

I really need to go shopping for some new shoes, apples, carrots, and SnickerPoodles for Theodora and Suzy Q. Maybe Bill needs to go shopping for a new cowboy hat or a bandana. I will ask him. Maybe that will work.

Dusty had his head outside the stall door when Farmer Bill rounded the corner. Farmer Bill had black hair and blue eyes, with a dimple in his chin. It was hard to tell exactly how tall Farmer Bill was because he wore a large cowboy hat, which always made him taller. He wore a red bandana, plaid shirt, and blue jeans with a silver polished belt buckle with the Green Apple Farm logo on it. His brown leather boots were polished, shiny and worn with silver spurs. Farmer Bill stopped in the middle of a whistle.

"Something wrong? Are you okay?" Farmer Bill asked Dusty.

Dusty replied, "My feet hurt and my shoes are not shiny anymore. Can we go shopping for some new shoes and maybe

some more apples and carrots from the Everything Store? The shoes you bought from the other store are not comfortable or shiny, and they are already worn and broken. Can we go today, please, and maybe could we get some apples and carrots, the good ones? You could get something like a new hat or a bandana. Maybe we could get some SnickerPoodles for Theodora and Suzy Q?"

Farmer Bill patted him, stroked his mane, put his saddle on him, and picked up his reins. Dusty just kept his head down.

Farmer Bill shook his head and said, "I'm sorry, but I ran out of time to go to the Everything Store to get your favorites. These will just have to do."

Dusty turned around to face the wall and hit Farmer Bill with his tail.

Farmer Bill thought, *I can't believe it. I am already late in getting out to the pasture, and I have a lot of work to do besides riding around on an unhappy horse.*

Farmer Bill pulled the reins, turned Dusty around and said, "I'm sorry, but we have to go." He threw the reins over the saddle, put his foot in the stirrup and hoisted himself up in the saddle.

Farmer Bill reached down and stroked his mane and said, "I am sorry I did not make time to get your favorite things at your favorite store. You know I like the store too because my hat, boots, jeans, gloves, bandana—well, I guess just about everything I am wearing today came from there."

Farmer Bill continued, "Can we talk about this later today, maybe over oats, apples and carrots? We have a lot of work to do, and it is going to be a long day if you don't cooperate and we don't get started."

Dusty answered, "Okay, I will take you where you need to go today, but it won't be easy. I love those shiny shoes and they are comfortable."

"We don't have time to get your trailer, comb your mane and tail, and get you presentable to go to town today," Farmer Bill responded. "If we can just get our work done today, tonight we will discuss this situation over oats, apples, and carrots."

“Okay, but we have to shake on it,” Dusty said.

“But I am already up in the saddle. Can we pretend we agreed on it?” asked Farmer Bill.

Dusty tossed his mane. “No, we have to shake on it. Do you want me to pretend we had a talk? You have to get down and shake my leg”

“Okay, okay, I am getting down,” said Farmer Bill. He stood in front of Dusty. Dusty lifted his left front foot, and Farmer Bill shook his leg. “Feel better now?” he asked.

“Yes,” Dusty answered.

Farmer Bill got back up in the saddle and slowly started down the lane to the first row of fences. Dusty didn’t walk or canter as he usually did, but he was putting his best effort into it. Farmer Bill got down and walked the fence row. He repaired the gate that was loose. Farmer Bill took his reins and got back in the saddle, and they walked through the gate. They continued checking fences and finally reached the creek.

Dusty loved the creek. He loved to make a big splash, and when he was feeling silly, he tried to dump Farmer Bill in the creek. Today, Dusty just walked down the slope and into the creek.

“What’s wrong?” Farmer Bill asked.

Dusty answered, “I got mud on my hoofs and my shoes don’t shine anymore. Could we go or are you going to take an hour-long nap?”

“We will go,” answered Farmer Bill with a sigh.

They finished their work and headed back to the barn. When Dusty saw where he was going, he hurried even more.

They walked down to Dusty’s stall, and Farmer Bill opened his door. He reached for a towel and started rubbing Dusty’s feet. Dusty lifted his left foot, and he reminded Farmer Bill that they had a talk coming over oats, apples, and carrots. Farmer Bill shook his head as he worked his way around Dusty’s four legs, drying and rubbing his feet.

“Apples and carrots are coming, and oats are waiting,” said Farmer Bill.

Dusty raised his head. "Make sure they are the good ones or we won't have much to talk about."

Farmer Bill shook his head and shut the bottom door so Dusty could put his head out and catch the evening breeze. Maybe it would calm him down.

As Farmer Bill walked toward the house, he thought about Dusty. *He is a good horse, a hardworking horse, and a part of the family. Theodora loves sleeping in his hay, and I often find Suzy Q there as well. I even found a queen of hearts card when I was cleaning out his stall.*

Theodora and Suzy Q greeted Farmer Bill at the door of the cookhouse. They asked him to please check on Dusty. "He is not feeling well today."

Farmer Bill answered, "I know." "His feet hurt, and Dusty said he needs a new pair of pretty shoes, apples, carrots, and SnickerPoodles, your favorite animal treats, from the Everything Store."

Theodora rubbed his legs, and Suzy Q stood still so she could hear all the details. Farmer Bill gave them an extra hug and kiss along with a SnickerPoodle and asked them to go down to the barn while he hunted for Dusty's favorite apples. The Everything Store had a sticker on each apple. He looked through the apple bowl and found two apples and one long carrot with a frilly top with stickers from the store on them.

Farmer Bill thought, *Boy am I in luck. This is enough to get us talking about shoes, apples, and carrots.* He put them in a brown bag, grabbed a bottle of water and headed toward the barn. He started whistling so Dusty would know that he was coming. He heard the rustling of hay and soon saw Dusty's head hanging out the door. His eyes looked tired as he stood waiting. Farmer Bill began to sing the Everything Store jingle, and Dusty's ears perked up.

> "Everything Store, shopping for all,
> Come one, come all,
> Come on down and shop at the Everything Store."

Dusty looked up and saw the brown bag as Farmer Bill shook it. "I found some apples and carrots for you."

Dusty tossed his mane. "Really? Let me see."

Farmer Bill opened the door and walked in and sat down on his stool. Dusty moved closer to him and smelled the bag. He said, "It smells like apples and it smells like carrots—can it be? Are there any shoes?" he asked excitedly.

Farmer Bill shook his head and said, "No shoes, but we have apples and carrots so we can talk. Right, remember? We shook on it."

Dusty lifted his foot and answered, "Yes, we did."

"Look, I found two apples and one carrot," exclaimed Farmer Bill.

Farmer Bill cleaned the apple and asked Dusty if he wanted the apple cut into pieces. Dusty nodded his head.

He began to cut the apple and Dusty seemed to calm down. Farmer Bill gave him his first piece without saying a word.

Farmer Bill looked into Dusty's eyes and said, "I just want you to know I am really sorry I did not get your favorite things last time. I was trying to get to the store before they closed, but we had so much work to do that I did not get there in time, so I went to the other store."

Dusty answered with a sad look, "I know, but I didn't like walking around in these old shoes because they hurt my feet."

"Maybe no card game tonight," Farmer Bill said with a big grin.

"What are you talking about? What card game?" Dusty asked with a smile.

Dusty nudged his hand, and Farmer Bill gave him the carrot and another apple piece. He took it and chewed it as if it were the last one he would ever get.

Farmer Bill said, "It is too late tonight, but we could go tomorrow evening and look for your shoes, apples, and carrots. I brought you all the apples and carrots we had."

Dusty asked, "Did you say *we* could go? Not just you but I could go, too?"

Farmer Bill nodded.

Dusty was so excited that all he could say was, "Wow! Wow, what a plan. How do we do it, and when?"

"We finished the south side of the pasture today, so we only have to do the north side tomorrow. If we can be back in the barn by midafternoon, then we will have time to rub your feet, brush your tail, and get you ready for the horse trailer to take you to town. What do you think so far?" asked Farmer Bill.

"I like it," Dusty answered.

"Once we get to the Everything Store, then I can go in and get your things. We will be there before the store closes, and I promise you, you will have an apple before we leave the parking lot. What do you think, is it a plan?" Farmer Bill asked.

Dusty stood still and said nothing.

"Dusty, what's wrong? Don't you think it will work? What do you not like about it?" Farmer Bill asked.

Dusty looked at him and said, "I want to go *inside* the store to shop, just like you do. I want to try on my shoes, pick out my own apples and carrots and SnickerPoodles for Theodora and Suzy Q."

Farmer Bill looked at Dusty in disbelief. "Are you kidding me? Horses can't shop in stores. They can go in a trailer and wait in the parking lot, but they can't go into the store. There are rules and regulations."

"So?" Dusty answered.

"Dusty, you can't go into the store, and even if we got in the front door, they would escort us right out. Horses are not allowed in the store. It just won't work," Farmer Bill said firmly.

Dusty said, "I have a plan. It might work and it might not, but we don't know if we don't try."

"Are you going to tell me your plan, or are you going to surprise me?" Farmer Bill asked in disbelief.

Dusty looked at him as Farmer Bill cut another piece. "We will get ready to go tomorrow afternoon. I will put on my best horse outfit, and we will go to the Everything Store. I will take it from there."

"We will be asked to leave," Farmer Bill said.

"Oh, I know we will be asked to leave, but we won't be there long. If my plan works, I will get my shoes, apples, carrots, SnickerPoodles, and maybe a picture or two. Don't you think we could hang the pictures here in my stall so I can remember what it was like to go shopping?" Dusty asked.

"Sure," Farmer Bill answered. "Now let me rub you down so you can rest and be ready to go to the north pasture in the morning."

Dusty gave Farmer Bill his left front foot and Farmer Bill began to work on getting all the debris out of his shoe. He kept a steady hand, cleaning, brushing, and rubbing liniment on Dusty's feet and legs. Farmer Bill finished his rubdown and patted him goodnight and wished him sweet dreams.

"Get a good night's sleep. Tomorrow is the big day. Horse shopping—I can only imagine," Farmer Bill said with a grin.

The Next Day

Johnny Bob decided he needed some apples and caramel to make caramel apples, so off to the Everything Store he went with his grandparents. He walked into the Everything Store and stopped. Right in front of him stood a horse and a man holding his reins. They both stood as still as statues.

"Look! It's a horse standing in the store," said Johnny Bob, a curious six-year-old boy with red hair, blue eyes and freckles that crisscrossed his nose. He pushed up his blue-green glasses while tugging Grandpa's arm.

The manager, Alan, ran up to the man and his horse, shook his head excitedly and sputtered, out of breath, "You can't bring your horse into the store. You need to leave him outside. There is a post you can tie him to, or you can use the shopping cart return post to tie his reins. We had another man who tied his horse to the post in the shopping cart return. He did not bring his horse into the store." The manager pushed up his glasses, put his hands on his hips, and planted his feet firmly in front of the man.

Farmer Bill smiled and said, "Oh, he won't be a bother. He just wants to pick up a few things in the store."

The manager looked at the man and his horse and shook his head. He said, "Horses can't shop in the store. *We have rules.*"

Farmer Bill said, "I know the rules, but you see, it is very important to him that he shops in his favorite store. He wants to shop for pretty shoes, apples, carrots, and SnickerPoodles. Dusty is his name."

People were beginning to gather around. Farmer Bill and Dusty didn't move.

Alan stammered, "Rules—we have rules! He is not allowed in the store. Why does he think he can shop like everyone else, people that is! Do you see any other horses shopping in here? Give me a break."

While Farmer Bill and Alan were arguing, Johnny Bob said to his grandparents, "Can we go over and see if I can talk to the horse?"

"Yes, we will all go," answered Grandpa.

Johnny Bob walked over to the horse, looked at him, and said, "Hi, I'm Johnny Bob."

Dusty raised his left foot and answered, "Hi, I'm Dusty. Pleased to meet you. You can shake my foot. It's okay."

Johnny Bob reached down and shook his foot. Dusty answered with a grin, "A good shake."

Johnny Bob said, "I have never seen a horse inside of a store before. What are you doing?"

Dusty smiled his big wide grin and said, "Shopping."

"Shopping? Shopping for what?" asked Johnny Bob.

Dusty answered, "Pretty shoes, apples, carrots, and SnickerPoodles."

Johnny Bob pointed his finger toward the man in the hat and asked, "But why are you shopping and not, um, him?"

Dusty answered, "His name is Bill. On the farm, we call him Farmer Bill."

"But why isn't Farmer Bill shopping for you?" Johnny Bob asked as he stroked Dusty's mane.

"I so wanted to go inside the store and see what it was all about. I only get to see from outside of the trailer window. I wanted to walk inside the store, see the people, hear the music, and see all the wonderful things to buy. I knew we might not get in because of rules and regulations. I don't mean to break rules or regulations."

Johnny Bob looked at Dusty with an intent face and said, "You don't always get everything you want when you want it. Rules and regulations are in place to protect people."

"I know," said Dusty, "and I mean no harm to anyone. It won't

take long to shop, and I will be very careful not to break anything. I just thought maybe one time I could shop in the store. Would you go with me and help me pick out pretty shoes, apples, carrots, and SnickerPoodles?" Dusty asked.

Johnny Bob looked at Dusty and said, "If you get to go shopping and it's all right that my grandparents go with us, I will help you. You have not even started shopping yet!"

"I know," answered Dusty, "but already I am news on all the different airwaves. Look at all of those people taking pictures and typing on their phones while Farmer Bill and the manager argue over whether I get to stay or go."

Dusty nudged Johnny Bob and said, "Walk with me over to Farmer Bill, and I will introduce you if we can get a word in edgewise. Bring your grandparents with you."

"Okay," said Johnny Bob.

Dusty, Johnny Bob, and his grandparents walked a few steps over to Farmer Bill and the manager. Dusty put his head into Farmer Bill's arm. Farmer Bill turned around and looked in surprise at Dusty, Johnny Bob, and his grandparents.

Dusty said, "These are my new friends, Johnny Bob and his grandparents. They can help me shop."

Farmer Bill turned back to the store manager, Alan, explaining, "Yes, Dusty is a very special horse. He can talk, and he likes to eat apples and carrots and wear pretty shoes—all from the Everything Store. We are wasting time that he could be shopping. With help from Johnny Bob and his grandparents, Dusty could be shopping and out of here in a little bit. Look outside; there are news reporters with cameras and they are starting to come in. Alan, you and the Everything Store will be on the news and lots of airwaves, which could go around the world. Just think how much news you and the store will get out of this."

Farmer Bill pulled Dusty's reins and started walking over to the apples and carrots. He patted Dusty and said, "You can pick out the ones you want. I know you have your eyes on them. Come on, everyone; let's help Dusty pick out pretty shoes, apples, carrots, and SnickerPoodles."

Shoppers began to murmur. "Look, he found the apples; Johnny Bob is putting them into a sack. Now the carrots go in another sack."

Shoppers were whispering. "Wait, he is walking over to the pet aisle. What do you think he is doing over there?"

"Look, Johnny Bob is taking one and now two bags of SnickerPoodles. Who gets those?"

Johnny Bob turned and answered, "The cat and dog!"

"So far, Dusty has apples, carrots, and SnickerPoodles."

"He is still shopping and still inside the store. Oh, I can't believe it. Are you sure you got his picture—a good picture?" shoppers were saying to each other.

Everyone continued talking and following Dusty, Farmer Bill, Johnny Bob, and his grandparents. "Look, he is on the move again; oh look, he stopped so the children could pet him. Isn't this the best? Now he is

moving again. Hurry, keep up. We don't want to lose our place, or we won't get to see what's going on because of all the shoppers."

"He has found the shoes. Oh, my gosh, there are so many pretty shoes. He is looking at the silver ones—they're off the shelf. Now what is he doing?"

"A pair of boots, yellow boots with polka dots. How cute is that? Johnny Bob sure has his hands full."

"Look," one of the shoppers said and pointed their finger, "Farmer Bill got a yellow bandana to go with Dusty's yellow boots with polka dots. How cute is that!"

Farmer Bill looked at Dusty and asked, “Anything else?”

“I am good,” answered Dusty. Dusty turned and said to all the people, “Thank you so much for the most special day in my life. I got to go shopping at my favorite store and pick out my very own pretty shoes, apples, carrots, and SnickerPoodles for the cat and dog. Even Farmer Bill got a bandana to match my boots. Oh, what fun we will have on the farm. I want you to know that I will never forget this day in all of my life.”

He grinned his full grin with all of his teeth showing, bowed his head, and gave a soft neigh. “I also want to thank the Everything Store and Alan the manager for letting me shop at the store. Now it is time for me to go. I hope you enjoyed this day as much as I did.”

All the people applauded and made room for Farmer Bill to walk to the checkout to pay for Dusty’s purchases. Farmer Bill paid for the purchases and walked to the front door of the store. He stopped and waved to everyone and said, “Thank you for making Dusty’s day and for shopping with him at the Everything Store.”

Dusty bowed his head, and they walked out the door with Farmer Bill holding Dusty's reins. Johnny Bob and his grandparents walked alongside of Farmer Bill. They shook hands, and Farmer Bill took the pretty shoes, apples, carrots, and SnickerPoodles and put them into Dusty's trailer.

Johnny Bob shook Dusty's leg and said "Thank you for making my day. I had the best shopping time ever."

Farmer Bill pulled an apple out of the bag and said to Johnny Bob, "I always give Dusty an apple at the Everything Store. Thanks for helping Dusty shop for his pretty shoes, apples, carrots, and SnickerPoodles for Theodora and Suzy Q. He will never forget you or this day."

"I won't, either," said Johnny Bob.

"Come and see me soon, Johnny Bob!" Dusty grinned. "I will, I promise" answered Johnny Bob.

Dusty nudged Farmer Bill and said with a great big smile, "Thank you! It was the best day ever to go shopping at the Everything Store. I will never forget it."

"Me neither," said Farmer Bill.

Farmer Bill nodded his head and said, "We best be going before we get mobbed by all the media. Let's get you in the trailer."

"There is just one more thing," Dusty said.

"What?" asked Farmer Bill.

"A cherry limeade!" Dusty exclaimed.

"A cherry limeade!" said Farmer Bill.

"Could we stop on our way home at our favorite drive-in for a cherry limeade, please, pretty please?" Dusty pleaded.

"You know sometimes when we finish the north pasture before we go to the barn, we ride over to the drive-in and get a cherry limeade. It is always so much fun. We get the great big one—you know, the one you get that makes all of those slurping sounds. You share some of it but not all. You always talk with me about taking care of my teeth! One cherry limeade is not going to ruin my teeth. But then all the kids, adults, and the carhops gather around and pet me, and it makes it so nice. Please can we go?"

“A cherry limeade it is,” said Farmer Bill. Dusty slurped the cherry limeade with a big grin all over his face!

“Shopping, I got to go shopping. What a day, and now a cherry limeade!” Dusty exclaimed.

Everyone just stood by and said, “Did you ever see the like!”

CPSIA information can be obtained
at www.ICGtesting.com
Printed in the USA
LVOW05*2023180917
549162LV00015B/61/P